Ragged Mountain Revelry

Christopher Hill Morse

"Ragged Mountain Revelry" is written and illustrated by Christopher Hill Morse. It is represented in the collection of The Northeast Children's Literature Collection. The illustrations are from original etchings printed by hand in color. They represent an effort of more than ten years. They are represented in the collections of The Smithsonian Institution, The Hunterdon Museum of Art, The New Hampshire State Council on the Arts, and have been represented in National shows such as the 45th Annual National Print Exhibition, 2001 North American Print Exhibition, 2000 Pacific States Biennial National Print Exhibition, Artlink's 20th National Print Exhibition, 2000 Mayfair National Art Competition, Prints USA 1999, The 2nd Mid-Atlantic Small Print Exhibition, Albany Print Club's 20th National Print Exhibition, and others.

"Ragged Mountain Revelry" Copyright © 2000 published and printed by The Oculus Press, RR 1 Box 690, Grafton, NH, USA 03240.

Library of Congress Catalog Card Number: 00-90315

ISBN 0-9678775-0-4

"Good things can happen

in the pursuit of happiness!"

Christopher Hill Morse, 2000

To David and Mark,

Christopher and Morse

July 6, 2001

Prologue

Somewhere not far from your own back yard you may find a place that lets you feel comfortable with the world being just what it is, a place that has been crafted by nature itself, somewhere that has escaped the momentum of progress. Someday, you may have a voice in allowing it to be special for your grandchildren and for their grandchildren as well. In this way you may share love and a sense of place.

Stand on the high ledges of Ragged Mountain and see the glacial erratic, a great stone carried there by the moving sheet of ice that filled the valley ten thousand years ago. Imagine the day the melting ice gently set the rock on the ledge on which it rests. The contours of the rest of the valley remain hidden. In a rush, let your thoughts melt the expanse once filled with ice to the tiny pond that exists today. Imagine the grass taking hold as the rocks dissolve. This feeling for the wheels of time, shared with me by my mother, who studied geology, I will share with my grandchildren someday. This is a story about the protection of this wilderness, told from the animals' point of view.

Animated by the crows: there is magic in the moment when animals start off from a pause together which helps me believe that all things are connected.

Ragged Mountain is a bowl of peaks and ridges that surrounds a tiny pond within the land owned by Ragged Mountain Fish and Game Club. It enjoys a view of Mount Kearsarge, located within one of New Hampshire's beautiful state parks. On the outside of the bowl is a fine ski area with a cluster development. The drastic changes to the wilderness there may have been the catalyst that got land owners in the area to want their land to remain wilderness. Nineteen different land owners, one of which was Ragged Mountain Fish and Game Club, banded together with The Society for the Protection of New Hampshire Forests to put some five thousand acres into a protective easement, preserving the entire south face of the mountain forever.

Kendra is a little girl who has enjoyed the opportunity of growing up at Ragged Mountain Fish and Game Club, where her father grew up and where her grandparents live. The Fish and Game Club is a tiny community of fifty families. It is unusual in that none of them own the land on which their homes sit. The land, some fifteen hundred acres, is owned by all of them cooperatively. Most of it is wilderness. The land is designated as a tree farm, and the club follows a sustained forestry plan. Ragged Mountain Fish and Game Club will celebrate its centennial in 2001. Growing up in a community of cooperative land ownership is a perfect way to learn about land stewardship. We share in taking care of our world and never really possess it.

We set our story after the efforts to protect the wilderness have been underway for some years. The

Fish and Game Club must decide if they will join in and forever designate most of their land as wilderness. The entire community was involved.

Kendra's family was no exception. Her uncle had already been working with neighboring land owners. Her parents used their art business to help people appreciate the beauty of nature. One of her grandfathers did all the legal work <u>pro</u> <u>bono</u>, a phrase Kendra found out later meant "for free."

The story takes artistic license by allowing Kendra, whose birth inspired the creation of this story, to zoom back in time to enjoy the moment. It is told with the energy that flowed through everyone on the day that it made sense to make history.

Becoming a Part

Kendra lived in a tiny village a thousand feet up on the side of Ragged Mountain. The village was surrounded by the woods. She had become familiar with the woods around her house by exploring with her friends and taking walks with her family.

Kendra would go to the woods when she wanted to be alone. At first, when she went into the woods her head was full of thoughts; she just needed to find some space for herself. This time alone gave her a chance to think for herself and sort out how she felt about many things.

Soon Kendra became fascinated that so much changed in the woods with shifts in the weather and with the passing seasons. She found new reasons for her walks. Kendra enjoyed learning when to expect the return of different species of migrating birds. Her favorite was the rowdy announcement that spring had arrived, proclaimed by the returning flock of redwing blackbirds. Oak-a-lee, oak-a-lee, they would sing, finding her bird feeder even before the ice was out of the pond. She soon learned when particular wild flowers emerge, such as the skunk cabbage poking through the crusty snow, followed by the wintergreen and the uncoiling fiddleheads.

Kendra was beginning to take the life of the forest to heart. She was in a transition from just observing things to becoming part of them.

She found being accepted back into the woods was something that she just couldn't hurry. A small detail could lead her to forget herself for a moment and feel the whole wilderness experience. Everything lived there in constantly changing conditions of wind, rain, and the passing seasons. She was immersed in these changes. There was harmony in the life of the forest. She was accepting the woods on its own terms. Her life was part of the rhythm there.

Kendra had learned to reintroduce herself to the woods by first going to a favorite place that had a rock to sit on, moss that felt soft to her feet, and a spring. There she could talk out all that was on her mind. When she felt she was accepted as part of the woods again, Kendra would treat herself to a drink from the spring running clean and pure off the mountain.

As she would stand back up from her drink at the spring with the cold water still running down her throat, she found that she could hear the songs of the birds and the hush of the wind through the trees. She could enjoy the moment.

Recently, Kendra had the future of the forest on her mind. The forest was something that she believed would always be there. It seemed so permanent.

The adults of her village were thinking of joining in a grand agreement with other land owners to protect all the woods on their side of the mountain. It was called an easement. Kendra learned that this required anyone who might own the land in the future to keep the woods protected.

There were many people and properties involved and many details to work out. They had to decide the extent of the protected wilderness, and how the woods could be used. They had to try to respect the opinions and feelings of everyone. The whole village was involved.

These days, when Kendra was alone at her special place, she talked about the future of the woods. How wonderful it would be to protect it forever! As she talked about all this, she became aware that other ears were listening...

At first she noticed just the squirrels, cocking their heads and sneaking up closer. Soon the birds seemed to take an interest in what she was saying. Kendra became convinced that the animals were able to understand. It seemed to her that they took much more interest in her words when her words were about their woods. The squirrels were coming closer. The birds only sang when she was not talking.

Kendra experimented with this to be sure. She would try to trick the birds by starting to talk about the woods as soon as they started a song. They would stop at once, in the middle of a song sometimes. When Kendra would change the subject and talk about school or a favorite book, the animals would go back to what they had been doing before.

When she began to talk about the woods, the animals came closer and became silent. She knew that they understood. Kendra felt even more a part of the woods.

Kendra told the animals about each parcel of land that was promised to the protection of the ease-ment. Each time she shared a detail about a different parcel, the birds seemed to fly off in that di-rection. Kendra was sure that they were passing along the news.

The land including the bobcat ledges was one of the first parcels promised. Here was a boulder field riddled with caves where generations of bobcats had lived since the retreat of the glaciers. Other caves there made fine homes for the porcupines.

Soon the land along the back of the ridge trail was promised. This land was frequented by many deer and owls. They liked it because of the variety of trees and shrubs. The ground cover made it attractive to the mice and other small animals that fed the owl. The shrubs provided food for the deer through the long snowy winters.

Next to be included was the land surrounding an ancient field, older than the village itself. This place, where the deer would often bed down for the night, was called Mompey Pastures.

The Call

Like a rumor in a small town, the message was passed along from species to species. The whole community of animals was aware that the people were discussing the future of their woods. But none of the animals had heard Kendra mention the protection of the land under the high ledges. This was the location of the bear's favorite beech trees. The animals were concerned that these trees were left out of the protected woods. If the beech trees disappeared, the bear might not have enough to eat.

The date approached for the village to vote on whether or not to protect the woods. Kendra knew that it was now more important than ever to keep the animals informed. She told them when she heard new details.

Kendra found new tracks appearing around her favorite place. On her way there, she thought she saw the shapes of unfamiliar animals cautiously staying just on the edge of sight. More of the animals wanted to hear for themselves if the rumors about the protection of their home were true.

Among the animals, there was

much discussion going on as well. Many felt that the little girl was one of them. After all, she was talking directly to them. These animals wanted to convince the rest that they should make the girl an animal ambassador. This would allow them to end their eavesdropping, approach her directly, and even talk with her. Perhaps talking with Kendra directly could insure the protection of the beech trees. Other animals felt that they should be more cautious about such an important decision. The animals all knew there was much at risk.

Kendra no longer needed the first part of each visit to the woods for getting back in touch. She came ready.

The animals were always aware when a person had become attuned to the woods. People with their senses shut down sound loud to the animals. These people do not move with the rhythm of the woods. Animals find it ridiculous that humans can seem unaware of the life force around them. When a person has become part of the energy, the animals feel a sense of relief; around such a person the animals can go about their business.

The animals would joke among themselves about the humans and pretend not to be aware of each other. All the animals found this funny.

To make Kendra an ambassador, the animals would have to be convinced that she would never become separate again. The squirrels, at least, felt that she was ready.

Making the Case

Each animal had noticed something about Kendra that proved that her senses were already opened, that she was a part of the woods, no longer apart from them.

The skunk had seen how she had learned to feel the path with her feet so that she could walk at night without a flashlight. A path is harder than the soft duff of the forest floor. The path is indented, and with a little practice it is fairly easy to get around at night. Kendra had learned all the paths around her house by heart. She was comfortable and confident walking back home from Mompey Pastures, or from the meeting house after the games ended for the night. When you know where you are, the woods are not so dark.

The bear had seen her notice this year's abundant crop of beechnuts on his favorite trees, trees that were covered with his claw marks. He was sure that she imagined him up in the trees, harvesting the nuts. She seemed pleased to know that a good year for beechnuts, would be a good year for bears.

The birds too had noticed that Kendra kept track of when the wild flowers would bloom. They also noticed that she had learned to recognize different birds by their songs.

The deer had watched Kendra tasting the berries. She had learned how to find the sweetest wild strawberries early in the summer, and as the season passed, she learned about blueberries, raspberries, blackberries. She was quite particular in her choice of apples growing wild at Mompey Pastures, selecting only those that were crisp, red, and ripe.

Kendra surprised the deer when she showed up early one morning to pick apples. They noticed her feeling their beds in the matted grass at Mompey Pastures and finding them still warm, she stood up quickly and scanned the edge of the woods to see if the deer were still within sight.

The animals had many other stories that showed how Kendra had grown from just observing nature to finding her place within it. Even so, the most cautious of the animals still needed proof that Kendra remained a part of nature's balance when she was out of the woods. These animals wondered if she forgot about them when she went back inside her house.

The animals who believed in Kendra hoped that they could name her an ambassador. Then, if she gave them the good news that the adults had voted to protect the woods, they would be able to invite her to celebrate with them. However, there wasn't going to be time to properly decide to make Kendra an animal ambassador before the decision would be made about the future of the woods.

The date for the village to vote had arrived. This very night the adults would decide if they would join with their neighbors to protect the woods. The arrival of guests had made the ani-

mals suspicious. The speculation, as you might expect among animals, was wild.

Would the people protect habitat for all the animals? How could the animals make sure the people included the bear's favorite beech trees in the protected forest? All the other animals had excellent habitat within the protected land. If the animals waited to find out, it might be too late to make sure this part of the forest was included. How could they wait one more day?

A Simple Test

The animals' great anticipation gave the bear an opportunity. He always had a knack for getting to the point, making things happen. If the cautious animals needed proof that Kendra could be trusted as their ambassador, he had a way to find out if she kept the life of the forest in her heart when she was out of the woods.

The plan was simple. That night, while the adults were away at the meeting, the animals would all silently gather outside Kendra's house after she was asleep. If she had the qualities they required in an ambassador, she would sense that they were there; she would wake up and come to greet them. Even for the animals for whom procedure seemed important, the bear felt sure his plan could give them the necessary proof. The bear would try to gather everyone together.

He was discouraged at first. At the spring near the foot of the mountain, the first animal he found was the owl. The owl had always been critical of just about anything that the bear did. Owls do everything with stealth, not a strong suit for bears, and the owl's constant probing questions were more than any bear could tolerate. Still, the bear felt that he was on a mission and was surprised and delighted when the owl found merit in his plan. The owl flew ahead to help the bear find the other animals. As it was the bear's plan, the owl allowed him to lay it out for the rest.

The Gathering

The bear chose a path that took them through the habitats of all the animals. They went first to the watering holes. Two of them were vernal pools and disappeared during the summer, but one provided water all year. The bear and the owl felt sure they would find deer there. From the watering holes, they proceeded to the bobcat ledges. Next they followed the ridge trail near the Killkare cabin high above the village. Then they circled down the inside of the mountain's bowl toward the pond. Many animals were gathered around the pond. With all the animals walking together they would cross over the bridge below the pond and silently parade to the last house in the village where Kendra lived.

The deer were easy to find and went along with the plan straight away. The owl and the deer all hung back as the bear tried to convince the bobcat. "Robert, I know that you are going to say no, but still, you need to hear the plan. Come along if you are curious."

The bear's plan worked. Even though the cat told them that he would never go along with a plan of the bear's, they knew Robert would be following.

The path that they had chosen was

easier for some of the animals than for others. From time to time, the bear had to stop to allow the slower animals to catch up. The animals did not ordinarily mingle together, and the wait was awkward. With the common interest in their woods they had formed a bond of sorts, but it was not easy. There was great history between them.

They became proud of each other for staying with the mission that night.

The bear waited only as long as it took for the last animal to catch up. Then he started on his way again. The porcupine never got a rest and was exhausted. There is nothing more bedraggled looking than an exhausted porcupine. Some of the other animals complained that the bear was insensitive. He did seem short tempered. He was not at all excited by the prospect of the woods being protected. The owl nicknamed the bear Gruff. The bear countered and nicknamed the owl Lofty. There was growing concern for the porcupine. The owl decided that at the next chance, he would champion the cause, stopping the procession at least long enough for the porcupine to get a rest.

The group continued to grow. On their way to the ridge trail, a weasel had joined them. Along the ridge trail, they happened upon a moose. Moose are very simple thinkers, so the bear had to explain everything twice. Many animals had joined the mission. There were rabbits, mice, raccoons, a fox, and even Robert the bobcat had joined the crowd.

A Meeting of Minds

Everyone was excited that the people would vote to protect their forest home. What a glorious night it would be. The bear just didn't seem to care. Lofty decided to confront him.

"We are all excited with the probability of a protected woods, and you, Gruff, seem like you are lost to the prospect. You are harsh and short and insensitive to all the smaller animals who are working so very hard to keep up. Either you have no joy in you, or you are lost in a singular search toward insouciance."

The wood turtle asked the owl if the phrase should be a singular search <u>for</u> insouciance. The owl explained that insouciance is a Zen-like state; if you realized you were there it was gone, that it was all in the search. The fox asked what insouciance was. The weasel explained that it was that state of mind where you were not worried about anything. "My African cousin the meerkat has a phrase for it. It is such a wonderful phrase..."

Before the weasel could finish, Lofty, now all pumped up with bravado for having confronted the bear, broke in, "My ignorant little weasel, for your information while you are similar in shape to your African friend, you are not in the same family at all. You are merely in the same order."

As quick as a wink, the bear was right up in the owl's face. "I am sure you realize, Lofty, that I am in the same order as the weasel, and that it was impolite of you to interrupt him.

"I can have no dissention in the ranks, so let me explain myself. You see me as Gruff, mean and insensitive. Does any one of you have any emotional energy saved up for the possibility that the humans might not vote to protect our woods? If that happens, you will be emotional wrecks. You will be upset for days or longer. I will carry on as usual.

"Hopefully the people will remember to protect habitat for all of us. I will be the first to be thrilled about the protection of our woods, as soon as I know it is so.

"You don't understand my own self concept. What you see as mean and insensitive, I see as being a model of efficiency."

The porcupine asked the moose "What is Zen?" "It's nothing," said the moose.

Getting Reacquainted

They walked for some time without saying a word. No one had known the bear thought about anything. Now, on finding out that he had a self concept and that he knew to which order each of the different animals belonged, they felt guilty that they had underestimated him. The owl chuckled to himself about the moose.

Finally, through the trees, they could see the sparkling of the moonlight on the pond. The turtle spoke. "Each individual is like a wave on this pond moved by the wind of our experience. We each come from a larger body and are interconnected to some extent. Yet we may try to pull away from the others. If an inspiring light

shines on us, then we reflect it back. When you get further away from the individual waves the separate reflections fuse into a single glow. We can hope that the beauty of our habitat will be the inspiring light for each person voting, and that they will reflect it back by deciding to protect it."

For the first time the bear was moved. "There is so little tangible evidence that people are capable of seeing beyond the scope of their own lives. When people decide to embrace things the way they are, by protecting a habitat such as our woods, which is a watershed and a forest, this demonstrates an unselfish sensitivity for the health of the habitat which we all must

share; <u>this</u> gives me the evidence I need to believe in them.

"I did not mean to dash all your hopes. I too hope that it all comes true. If that little girl convinces the adults to protect habitat for all of us, I promise to dance a jig with her in Mompey Pastures."

There was no mistaking when the bear was jubilant. He would bob and shake his head, stomp and shuffle his feet. He would bounce with a spring in his step. When he was a cub he would leap up and kick his feet together. Now, most often, he would roll back and forth on the ground kicking his legs in the air.

The animals would all delight in seeing the bear try to amuse the girl with a human dance. The bear knew that they would all hold him to it! Then, perhaps she would like to learn the steps to their own special dances. The thought of it did get them all excited.

They found many more animals around the pond. Gruff was particularly hoping that Kendra would be able to help. If only she could get to the meeting with the information about the important habitat before the adults voted...

They were just a short walk from the
house where Kendra lived.

Naming an Ambassador

Silently, they walked into the yard. They knew that Kendra would tell them the following day about how the adults had voted, but that might be too late to protect the beech woods. They all hoped that she would sense that they were there, wake up, and come to greet them. Then the animals of Ragged Mountain would have an ambassador.

It had been longer than any of them could remember since there had been a person with whom they could speak directly. The turtle believed the last animal ambassador at Ragged Mountain had been Mr. Mompey.

The animals were startled when a light went on. The door swung open. The animals gasped. There stood Kendra.

"Madam ambassador," the deer bowed, "There is a great task which you must shoulder for us. Significant habitat for the bear has been left out of the protected woods. The bear's favorite beech trees have not been included. These trees are important to the bears. Their trunks are scarred with generations of claw marks. Adult bears will train their cubs to harvest beechnuts on the same trees on which they had been taught. Without these trees, the bears might not have enough to eat."

Kendra hoped that she wasn't too late. She ran to the meeting house and got her parents' attention from the window. Quickly she explained about the bear's stand of beech trees. The project wouldn't be complete unless it included habitats for all the animals. Her parents realized that this important habitat _had_ been left out. Happily the adults hadn't voted yet. Kendra's information helped remind them of the importance of the beech woods. They decided to include the bear's favorite trees in the protected forest.

Kendra ran back home with the news for the animals. Proudly she told them that the adults had voted unanimously to protect the woods, including the bear's beech trees! She felt happy that she had succeeded in her first mission as the animals' ambassador.

Once again the deer bowed, "Madam ambassador, the bear would like to invite you to join him at a joyous dance in Mompey Pastures."

"I would be greatly honored. Thank you," Kendra announced as she joined the animals.

Each animal pretended not to notice the smile spreading across the face of the bear. If there is one thing that is true about the woods, it is this: if the bear is happy and has everything he wants, everybody is happy!

It seemed as if the hike to Mompey Pastures took no effort at all. The porcupine no longer looked bedraggled; it looked resplendent. The turtles no longer crawled; they scooted. All the animals had more energy than they knew what to do with, and so, they danced!

The Dance

Each animal found its own dance. They started with their own animal steps. The deer leaped and pranced. Gruff did his own thing, and then, as he had promised, he danced a jig with Kendra. The bear felt it showed proper respect for the new ambassador to dance a human dance with her. Next

Kendra danced with the bear's whole family.

The moose, whose natural step looked like a show horse trying to polka, also tried a few human dances. They had favored the tango, but found that they had a great talent for dancing the jitterbug. On all fours they did a hilarious old soft-shoe.

The bears found that an old flapper dance called the black bottom seemed to fit them just right. They gave it their own flair and called it "The Black Bottom Romp."

Each of the animals found some favorite steps. The raccoons pranced a ballet all their own. The rabbit taught the mice the bunny hop. The turtles stuck to their waltz. Somehow there was a rhythm for everyone. Finally, Kendra learned the joyful steps of each of the animals' special dances.

On this magic night, in the last pastures from the Mompey farm that had stood there hundreds of years ago, a long-dry well bubbled forth with cool refreshment. It was as if Mompey's spirit was dancing that night, too.

The Dream

There was no sleep for the animals that night. Kendra, however, found her limbs getting heavy. The pasture was soft enough. She lay on the grass.

Kendra felt certain somewhere else there were other animal ambassadors reassuring their animal friends with their support. In a moment of reverie, they might even speculate about her;

wondering who the newest animal ambassador could be.

She looked forward to having more stories of her own wilderness experiences to tell to friends who shared her interests. On her adventures she might even meet other animal ambassadors.

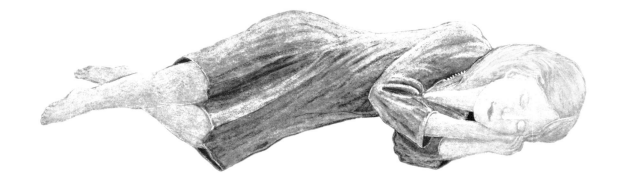

Kendra fell into a very special sleep. She was happy, through and through. She had found friendship through trust. She felt happy the woods were now protected. She was delighted the animals had made her their ambassa-

dor. She slept the sleep of friendship's security. Tonight, she would need no warmer blanket.

She drifted into a deep sleep. She dreamed of a magic flying back pack. With it she could explore the world and find friends with the 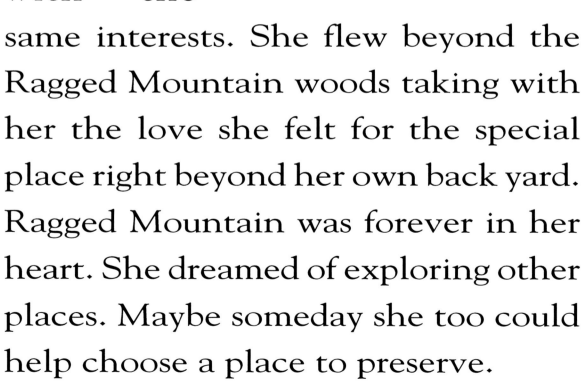 same interests. She flew beyond the Ragged Mountain woods taking with her the love she felt for the special place right beyond her own back yard. Ragged Mountain was forever in her heart. She dreamed of exploring other places. Maybe someday she too could help choose a place to preserve.

Kendra always had wanted to see the lands of our forebears, lands about which she had heard so much. She had her own vision of what these might be like. Kendra dreamed of four real bears stretching out the land as far as they wanted. She flew over the landscape with friends to camp at their favorite place on an island in a great lake.

The Search

Kendra's dog noticed that she was gone. After showing Kendra's mom and dad that Kendra was not in her bed, the dog quickly got them to follow her. It is very useful to have a dog when you need to find someone in the woods.

Kendra's parents were trying not to worry too much. They were reassured

that the dog seemed to know right

where to go.

It was harder than usual for the dog to follow Kendra's scent as it was now mixed with all the smells of the other animals. The dog worked hard and concentrated only on the little girl's scent.

Kendra now knew who she was dreaming about. The friends with the same interests, the friends who could take her to explore the lands of our forebears, were her parents. She felt their familiar hug.

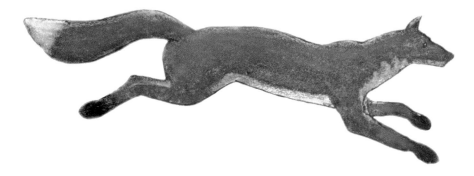

She opened her eyes as her father picked her up, and she smiled. "I had a dream that we will be good friends when I grow up," Kendra whispered.

"That's our dream as well," said her mom and dad.

The Visit

The next time Kendra went into the woods, she thanked the animals for including her in their celebration and particularly for teaching her their own special dances.

The animals assured her, "You will always be part of our community."

She asked Gruff, "Why don't you all come back with me to play in my village?" Kendra hoped that her new friends would come home with her. Some of the animals were skeptical, but Kendra made them feel so welcome that the they agreed to think about it. The animals noticed she seemed disappointed that they didn't go with her.

After Kendra went home, Gruff pointed out to the other animals that they each had things that they had

wondered about and wanted to try. When they had debated the pros and cons of playing in Kendra's village, their own routine seemed mundane. "Perhaps a short visit can give us some valuable objectivity" suggested Lofty. The animals decided they would go for a visit.

The next morning, with a gleam in their eyes and wearing smug little smiles, the animals showed up at Kendra's village to play. Kendra helped to get each of them set up with just the right equipment to do what they wanted to do.

Gruff found that fly fishing was introspective enough to suit him. It seemed to him that fishing was, as the owl had put it, "a singular search toward insouciance." Gruff loved the bewildered faces of the people as he pushed off in a canoe.

He was very traditional and preferred dry-fly fishing. He scoffed at the suggestion of nymphs.

The moose enjoyed meditating on the porch of the meeting house. He had a great deal of trouble getting in and out of the rocking chairs he found there. He often tipped over while trying to put his legs up on the railing. But once he got settled, he would relax for hours. He felt centered while he was watching the stars. He concentrated on his breathing and the sounds of the night. Sometimes it seemed like the whole world was responding to him. He left before daylight brought out all the busy people.

He understood Zen well enough for a moose.

Some things worked better than others. Contrary to what you might think, kite flying turned out to be a great frustration to the robin. It was too detached from the actual expression of flight. "It lacks direct control," he complained. It struck him as funny that his explanation sounded like an artist he had once heard describing his preference for painting over printmaking.

The bears turned out to be excellent tennis players. It upset the humans when they realized that what appeared to be clumsy bear er-  rors were actually careful reenactments of all the things that human tennis players did wrong. The bears were far too amused by the humans' mistakes to offer them much help in the way of coaching. Although the bears courte- ously swept the court after they played, some of the humans complained about the bears' lack of proper attire.

Going Back Home

The animals all enjoyed trying out a thing or two from the human world, but they knew that what they did they did best back in their own familiar territory. It had been nice to get to know the people a little better, but the animals knew it was time to go back home to their own protected woods.

Every animal was perfect for one corner of the woods or another. Nature had designed each of them to be best suited for just what it most needed to do. Absorbed back into their own pursuits of happiness, the animals would face a secure future.

One by one, each animal came to thank Kendra for being such an excellent host and to tell her that they were headed back home to their woods. Each thanked her for being their ambassador. None of them expected that they would see her quite as often. They all hoped that they could get together again. Much was said about the glorious dance.

The bear was the last animal to find her. He seemed to want to avoid direct eye contact. But he had something important to say. "You must tell this story," he spoke most seriously as he leaned closer, "but you must tell it well enough so that those who hear it will be inspired to refer to their own success protecting the wilderness as "my Ragged Mountain story.'"

As Gruff sauntered back into the woods Kendra smiled and understood that the bear was truly a model of efficiency! She envisioned a heavenly library filled with books all titled "My Ragged Mountain Story," each about protecting a different wilderness habitat, each by a different author.

Perhaps one of them could be
written by you.

Epilogue

Twice this past summer my daughter Kendra and I camped in Mompey Pastures. We heard the chirping of the crickets. We heard a coyote far away howling at the moon. At our second camp out, we surprised some deer planning on sleeping there and heard the snort of a buck warning the other deer that there were people in their pastures.

Kendra is five years old. I hope that this story can keep her interested in learning about nature. I hope that she enjoys the fascinating variety of life. It takes vision to protect the environment.

To find out whether there was anything really extraordinary about Yellowstone, Congress sent two artists, William Henry Jackson, a photographer, and Thomas Moran, a painter, to explore the area and make a visual report. Their powerful art convinced Congress that Yellowstone should be preserved for all future generations to share. I hope my Ragged Mountain story can also serve as inspiration for others.

Protecting the land on Ragged Mountain involved many people and properties. Yellowstone, however, was designated protected land in a day when our forebears could extend the boundaries of our public lands as far as they wanted. The people who laid out Yellowstone simply drove a stake in the ground and rode for miles in one direction. When it seemed far enough, they drove another stake in the ground, and turned in a new direction. By the time they had gone all the way around, they had designated over a million acres as America's first national park. It will never be that easy again.

A thousand times while I have been demonstrating at art shows Kendra has heard me say that by exploring the lands of our forebears, we gain valuable objectivity by getting some distance from the circumstances of our daily routine. With this objectivity, we can weather any type of personal storm.

Wilderness can open up our senses. Much of our daily life goes unexamined, yet in time our connection to the wilderness lets us discover more about our own nature, and creates memory. With just the scent of a spruce tree or the song of a white throated sparrow, the memory of these places rushes back to mind.

The wilderness is everybody's family heirloom.

By being in touch with all those places left in our care, we will have a better idea of how to care for them and this focus may help us find the energy needed to preserve additional important habitat.

All of us are caretakers of our world. What we can learn about those things left in our care will help us have a positive influence on the future. It is important to realize the vitality in the variety of life. We are part of a thriving planet. This is the perspective I offer to my children. I am happy to share it with you.

Christopher Hill Morse, 2000